D0469958

PAW PATROL
THE MIGHTY MOVIE

# POWER UP, PUPS!

by Melissa Lagonegro

illustrated by Dave Aikins

Random House 🏠 New York

Everyone is excited
in Adventure City.
They are waiting to see
a meteor shower!

The PAW Patrol watches
from the tower.
They see a meteor!

It is bright.

It is big.

It is headed straight
for Adventure City!

The PAW Patrol gets
everyone to safety.
They clear the streets
before the meteor hits!

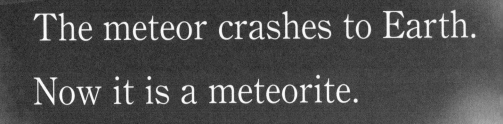

The meteor crashes to Earth.

Now it is a meteorite.

It makes a big crater
in the ground.
It glows and pulses
with energy!

Rocky uses his forklift
to move the meteorite.
The meteorite stops glowing.
Ryder inspects it.

Later, the pups fall asleep.
Skye wakes up.
She sees a bright light.
The meteorite is glowing
again!

Skye touches the meteorite.

It splits apart.

Energy crystals

are inside!

A crystal sticks
to Skye's collar.
It gives her superpowers.
Skye can fly!

Skye wakes the other pups.
Crystals attach
to their collars, too.
Now *they* have superpowers!

# Marshall shoots fireballs.

# Chase has super speed.

Zuma turns into water.

Rocky is a giant magnet.

# Rubble is a wrecking ball!

The pups get
new super uniforms.

# Now they are
# the Mighty Pups!